THE LEGEND OF THE TOOTH FAIRY

Written by John and Irene Lynch

Published by Lynch Legacy
ISBN: 978-1-7361183-1-3
Printed in the United States

Cover Art & Illustrated By: Penny Weber

This book is dedicated to our grandchildren:
Jack, Gracie, AJ, Brooklyn, and Carson. May you always
look at life through the eyes of a child.

Going to the Dentist

*Jill was sitting in the dentist chair
waiting for Dr. Jay. She thought to herself,
this would be the perfect time to ask him the
question that has puzzled her
and her friends.*

Maybe, he will know the answer.

Jill was eight years old and very curious about many things. She liked to ask questions about how and why things worked.

Dr. Jay entered the room with a big smile.

"Jill how are you today?" asked Dr. Jay. "I hope you've been brushing those beautiful teeth of yours!"

Dr. Jay is a very friendly man and always made Jill feel welcomed at his dentist's office.

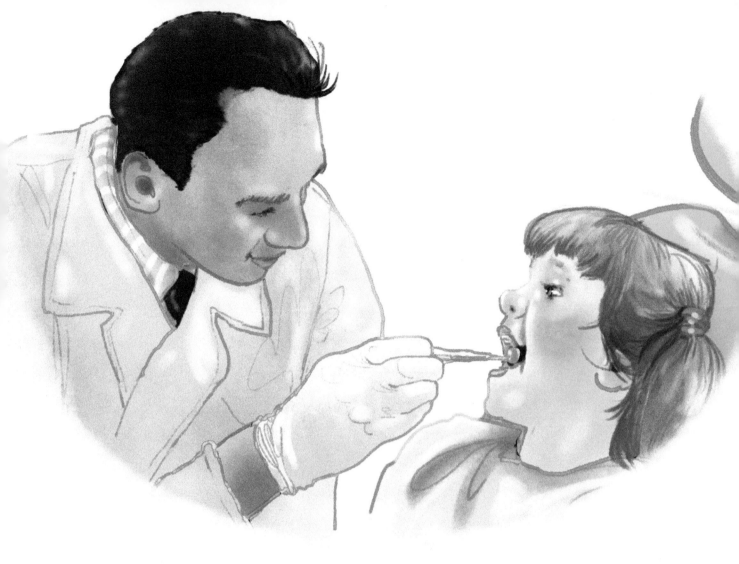

"I feel great," replied Jill, "and I always brush my teeth every day!"

When Dr. Jay checks on Jill's teeth, he uses a long metal tool with a mirror on the end of it so he can see the teeth way in the back of her mouth.

"Good," said Dr. Jay, "I can see that you've been brushing your teeth every day and flossing, too. Taking good care of your teeth is important!"

Jill decided the time was right and asked,
"Dr. Jay why does the tooth fairy collect teeth?
Why does she give us money?"

Dr. Jay scratched his head and said, "I don't know Jill, but when you find out,
please let me know." He handed her a new blue toothbrush
and a small tube of toothpaste.
As Jill headed for the door, she turned and said, "Thank you Dr. Jay,
and I'll be back soon when I find the answer."

Going to the Beach

It was a hot summer's day on Cape Cod and time for Jill, her two sisters, and friends to go for swimming lessons. Jill, Jenny, and Jackie walked to the end of the road with their babysitter, Chrissy and met their friends Johanna and Ben who walked with them.

They walked down the sandy path to the beach.
When the children and their babysitter reached the water, they waved to Bob the lifeguard. He was sitting high in his chair, watching the people swimming or playing in the water.
Bob was wearing a hat like the one you would wear to go hunting in the jungle. Bob often said, "I wear it to hunt big game!" then he would laugh.
He always made sure that
the children were safe when they went into the water.

Jill and Johanna watched as the older children lined up to begin their swimming lessons. Jenny, Ben, and Jackie decided to make sandcastles while they waited for their turn. The babysitter had carried a large canvas bag filled with sand buckets, shovels, and towels from home, and there were plenty for everyone. Jenny and Ben were six years old and Jackie was three. They loved spending time at the beach.

After a while a deep loud voice shouted, "Beginners, time for beginners!"
Lifeguard Bob then yelled, "Line up and get ready to swim."
They all ran to the lifeguard chair to line up. Johanna was first in line.
When it was time, she ran and dove into the water. Everyone followed.
Today was a great day for swimming.

Jill kept thinking about the tooth fairy during the lesson and wondering, why the tooth fairy collects teeth. She asked her sister, Jenny, "Do you know why the tooth fairy collects teeth?" Jenny said, "No, why don't you ask Lifeguard Bob? I bet he knows."

The lesson ended and Jill and Jenny got their towels to dry off. "Do you know why the tooth fairy collects teeth?" Jill asked Lifeguard Bob. The children began to crowd around. "No," answered Lifeguard Bob. "Why do you want to know?" he asked. "Just curious," answered Jill. Now all the children were wondering why.

Jill Asks Her Parents

As Jill was walking home with her sisters and babysitter, she saw her father painting the house. Jill asked, "Daddy why does the tooth fairy collect teeth?"

Her father thought for a moment and replied. "I really don't know Jill, but I'm sure there is a good reason for it.

Why don't you ask Mom?"

"Time for lunch!" called Mom. Jenny, Jackie and Dad headed for the sink to wash up for lunch. Jill walked into the kitchen and asked, "Mom why does the tooth fairy collect teeth?"

Her Mom smiled as if she knew and said, "We are going to Granddad's store this afternoon. I'm sure he knows the answer."

After lunch, Mom and Dad and the girls got into the car and drove to Granddad's store. Jill was the first one out of the vehicle. Grandma greeted the girls at the door. "Hi kids! Did you have fun at the beach today?"

"Yes!" exclaimed Jenny, "It was great!"

Jackie was the first to walk over to the candy counter. She spotted her Granddad coming down the stairs. "Hi gang," he waved.
"Would anyone like a piece of candy?"

Jill, Jenny, and Jackie crowded Granddad Potts as they tried to hug
him all at once. They all shouted, "Yes, Granddad!"

Each girl picked their favorite kind. Jill chose M&M's. Jenny picked
Gummy worms, and Jackie chose Necco wafers.
Mom picked her favorite nonpareils, and Dad asked
for a Reeses' peanut butter cup.

Jill then asked Granddad, "Why does the tooth fairy collect teeth?"
Granddad gave a big laugh.
"It's a long story," he said.

"Oh, please tell us Granddad," the girls pleaded.

"Ok', said Granddad, "Have a seat.".

The girls all took seats on the white bench near the candy counter.
Granddad began to tell them the story of the tooth fairy.

Granddad Potts' Story

Once upon a time in a tiny town called Floss there lived a mean
and evil king. His name was King DeKay. In the kingdom lived
many small fairies. The king didn't like the fairies because
they were always friendly and cheerful.

One day King DeKay called all the fairies to the castle.
He commanded, "In order for the fairies to live in my kingdom,
you must build me a white enamel road that glistens
when the sun shines on it." He knew that it would be an
impossible task and the fairies would have to leave
the tiny town of Floss.

Jill, Jenny, and Jackie crowded Granddad Potts as they tried to hug him all at once. They all shouted, "Yes, Granddad!"

Each girl picked their favorite kind. Jill chose M&M's. Jenny picked Gummy worms, and Jackie chose Necco wafers.
Mom picked her favorite nonpareils, and Dad asked for a Reeses' peanut butter cup.

Jill then asked Granddad, "Why does the tooth fairy collect teeth?"
Granddad gave a big laugh.
"It's a long story," he said.

"Oh, please tell us Granddad," the girls pleaded.

"Ok', said Granddad, "Have a seat.".

The girls all took seats on the white bench near the candy counter.
Granddad began to tell them the story of the tooth fairy.

Granddad Potts' Story

Once upon a time in a tiny town called Floss there lived a mean
and evil king. His name was King DeKay. In the kingdom lived
many small fairies. The king didn't like the fairies because
they were always friendly and cheerful.

One day King DeKay called all the fairies to the castle.
He commanded, "In order for the fairies to live in my kingdom,
you must build me a white enamel road that glistens
when the sun shines on it." He knew that it would be an
impossible task and the fairies would have to leave
the tiny town of Floss.

The fairies were quite upset because they knew of no such stone in the kingdom. The fairies searched the kingdom with no luck. They knew that they had to go beyond the Kingdom of Floss if they were to find this stone.

One fairy looked so hard that she didn't see
the other fairies had gone on ahead of her.
She was the littlest of all the fairies, and now
the tiny fairy was lost! She wanted to prove
to all the other fairies that she could help.
The small fairy traveled for many miles
until it was time to rest.
She rested during the day and
traveled by night.

She stopped by a large red barn and entered through
a crack in the wall.
The tiny fairy fell fast asleep.

Later in the day she woke up when a big girl picked her up from the bench where she was sleeping. The girl laughed in surprise and called her girlfriend to see what she had found.

The girls seemed very friendly, and when they smiled, the sun that came through the windows made their teeth shine. The fairy saw what she was searching for in the girl's mouth. The fairy explained to the girls what the mean King DeKay had demanded from the fairies of Floss.

"I wish we could help you," said one of the girls.

"Why, maybe you can!" said the fairy.
"Where can I get some white stones like
the ones you have in your mouth?"
The older girl said, "We have teeth in our mouth.
They are used to chew our food."

"Well I guess it doesn't help me if you need them to chew your food,"
the fairy sighed.

The younger girl then said, "Yes we can help!
When we are babies, we get our first teeth or baby teeth.
As we get bigger, we begin to lose our first teeth to
make way for new ones."

"That's right," said the older girl. "We can tell all our friends to give you their baby teeth when they fall out!"
"No, I can't just take their teeth. I should give them something in return," sighed the fairy.
They all sat quietly wondering what they could do.

Inside the red barn it began to get dark. The sun was resting on the edge of the sky. The last few rays of sunlight shown through the windows in the barn.
Just then one of the girls saw the sparkle of a coin. She shouted, "I've found the answer. We can give my friend, Carson, this coin for his tooth."

The fairy jumped up. "We have lots of coins in our wishing well, but we never knew what to do with them." The children and the fairy began to make their plans.

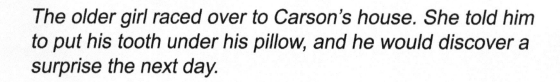

The older girl raced over to Carson's house. She told him to put his tooth under his pillow, and he would discover a surprise the next day.

That night the fairy bid the girls goodbye and thanked them for all their help. The girls promised that they would tell all the children that they know to put their baby teeth under their pillows when they fall out.

The fairy flew over to Carson's house and quietly entered his bedroom. She didn't want to wake the sleeping boy and carefully replaced the tooth under his pillow for a shiny coin. The fairy sped off to the kingdom of Floss to share her great fortune with the other fairies.

The littlest fairy arrived at the meeting house where all the fairies were assembled. They were all sad and quiet because none of them had found any enamel stones. The tiny fairy entered the room and exclaimed, "I have found the enamel stones for the king's road!"
She showed the fairies the small enamel tooth, and they all cheered!

The littlest fairy told them her story. All the fairies promised to go out every night and help collect the children's teeth. They hailed their littlest one a heroine for saving their home.

The next day King DeKay called all the fairies to the castle. In his deep and evil voice, he said,

"Have you found the stones of enamel that shine when the sun glistens on them?"

All the fairies cried at once, "Yes!"

The little fairy presented the king with the small enamel stone.

She said, "This is the first of many stones to come."

The king was surprised that they could do his impossible task, and he stormed off in a huff.

The fairies all cheered the littlest fairy.

"Hooray for the Tooth Fairy!"

Then Granddad said, "Till this day those fairies are still looking for children's teeth to finish the road to the king's castle. They travel at night while the king is sleeping, so he won't know where the fairies get their enamel stones."

Jenny turned to Jill and said, "I knew we should have asked Granddad. He knows everything!"
Jill agreed. She raced for the door. Grandma shouted, "Where are you going Jill?"
Jill turned and said, "I am going to tell Dr. Jay, Lifeguard Bob, and all the kids, the story of the Tooth Fairy!"

The End

Penny Weber is a full time illustrator from Long Island, New York.

She works on Photoshop creating digital
paintings and has illustrated many picture books
for the trade and educational markets.

Penny lives with her husband, three children
and their fat cat Tiger.

About the Authors

John and Irene Lynch are husband and wife and were married on February 24,1977. They have three daughters: Jill Lois Lynch Athridge, Jennifer Lee Lynch McCarron, and Jacquelyn Irene Lynch McCallister. They co-wrote this book in 1985, but it was not until Irene published her first book, "If Today You Hear His Voice," in 2020 that they finally completed and published "The Legend of the Tooth Fairy."

John Lynch taught elementary school students in grades second through sixth for forty-one years before he retired in 2013. He taught at the Balch School in Norwood, Massachusetts, for sixteen years before moving to Sarasota, Florida, with his family. John taught seventeen years at Ashton Elementary School and eight years at Tatum Ridge Elementary School.

Irene Lynch retired as an educator in 2013. She taught kindergarten and first grade at Philippi Shores Elementary School, was a Resource Teacher and Exceptional Student Education Liaison at Fruitville Elementary, an Assistant Principal at Venice Middle and Sarasota Middle School before becoming Principal at Epiphany Cathedral School.

CPSIA information can be obtained
at www.ICGtesting.com
Printed in the USA
LVHW072344190121
676816LV00004BA/20